TO MARSHA ROTH

VIKING
Published by Penguin Group
Penguin Young Readers Group, 345 Hudson Street, New York, New York 10014, U.S.A.
Penguin Group (Canada), 90 Eglinton Avenue East, Suite 700, Toronto, Ontario,
Canada M4P 2Y3 (a division of Pearson Penguin Canada Inc.)
Penguin Books Ltd, Registered Offices: 80 Strand, London WC2R 0RL, England

First published in 1978 by Greenwillow Books, an imprint of William Morrow & Company, Inc.
This edition published in 2007 by Viking, a division of Penguin Young Readers Group

10 9 8 7 6 5 4 3 2 1

THE LIBRARY OF CONGRESS HAS CATALOGED THE MULBERRY BOOKS EDITION AS FOLLOWS:
Keats, Ezra Jack. The Trip. [1. Halloween—Fiction] I. Title. PZ7.K2253Tr [E] 77-24907
ISBN 0-688-07328-X.
This edition ISBN 978-0-670-06195-2

Manufactured in China
Set in Bembo

EZRA JACK KEATS

The Trip

VIKING

Louie's family moved to a new neighborhood.
He didn't know anybody there.
No kids, no dogs, no cats.
And there weren't even any steps
in front of the door to sit on.
Louie sighed and went in.

He got an old shoebox.
He made a hole in the front,
cut out the back and part of the top,
and began to paste things inside.

He taped a piece of colored plastic on the top
of the box, and another piece on the end.
He hung his plane from the top, and closed the box.

Louie looked through the hole.

WOW!

Louie pretended he was flying his plane.
He flew higher and higher—over the moon.

He landed in his old
neighborhood.
It was very quiet.

He wandered around.
He could hear
his own footsteps.
Where was everybody?

He passed Roberto's old house—
and stopped suddenly.

He turned around
and ran—as fast
as he could.

He was trapped!

"Hey, wait—I know that tail!
It's the cat! And you're Roberto,
and that must be Amy and Archie."

They were his old friends!
"Surprise!" they yelled.
"Trick or treat!"

Louie took them for a ride
on his plane.
Everybody ran to the windows
to look at them.

It was time to go home.

Everyone was waving.

"Trick or treat!" Louie heard from far away.

"Come on, Louie," his mother was saying.
"Let me help you on with your costume."
They could hear the kids outside yelling,
"Trick or treat, trick or treat!"

Louie went outside
to join them.